Haran Travels To London

By Nalini Pillay

**For Haran and Zara,
May your curiosity open
doors to epic adventures.**

Telescope, Telescope
open your lens,
take me to London to
make some new friends.

Swish swash
the lens unravels,
and off to London
Haran travels.

London is the capital of England,
that's the country Haran
calls his homeland.

In his pockets are **pounds** and pence,
that's the money they use there
for every **expense**.

He lands in the middle
of **Trafalgar Square**,
where a **Union Jack**
flies in the air.

It's a **square** to honor
Horatio Nelson,
for the **Battle of Trafalgar**
he had won.

He wanders off to
Buckingham Palace,
where he meets a
girl called Alice.

They talk and play
outside the gate,
for the **changing** of
the guard they await.

The **Royal family** are
behind those gates,
having **afternoon tea**
with all their **mates**.

Off to **Hyde Park**
the two trot on,
the largest park
in all of London.

On to the big
red bus they hop,
as they make their
way to their **next stop**.

Tower Bridge goes
over the **Thames**,
like **London Bridge** from
which the **nursery rhyme** stems.

They watch as the
black cabs pass them by,
and catch a glimpse
of the **London Eye**.

Back on the **bus**
they once again **hop**,
as they make their
way to **another** stop.

The mighty **Big Ben**
hangs inside the clock tower,
as it **chimes** and **gongs**
every quarter hour.

They ride on down to
Westminster Abbey,
'It was once a **cathedral**,' they
were told by their **cabby**.

Off to the **Tower of London**
to see the crown jewels,
no touching allowed,
that's one of the rules.

It's **wonderful** to see all
these fascinating **sights**,
just **one place** left before it's night.

The **magnificent** cathedral
of St Paul stands **tall**,
as Haran and Alice slip
inside the **great hall**.

It's a **cathedral** designed
by Sir Christopher Wren,
and stands on the
highest hill in London.

It was a day of **adventure**
and **fun** all around,
and Haran is **thankful** for
the new **friend** he's found.

Time to head home
as the **day is done**,
another city on his list is done.

He **reaches** in his bag
and hands Alice a **band**,
it's the **friendship** kind,
that you wear on your hand.

They say their **goodbyes**
and promise to write,
as Alice **slowly** disappears out of **sight**.

19

He pulls out his **telescope**
from his bag in a flash,
as he passes a man eating
bangers and mash.

Telescope, Telescope
open your lens,
take me back home to
my **favorite** friends.

Swish swash
the lens unravels,
off to his home
Haran **travels.**

Interesting things

The national flag of the United Kingdom is known as the Union Jack

London is a city in England and England is part of the United Kingdom. London is the capital of England and the United Kingdom as a whole. The United Kingdom, also known as Great Britain is made up of 4 countries which include England, Northern Ireland, Scotland and Wales.

Bangers and Mash is a traditional dish of the UK and refers to sausages served with mashed potatoes. One possible reason why it is called bangers and mash is because during World War 1 when there was a shortage of meat, there were a number of fillers used when making sausages and one filler was water. So when the sausages were fried, the water in the sausage caused it to explode thereby giving it the name banger.

about the United Kingdom

Bubble and Squeak is a popular dish in the UK and is traditionally made from leftover food from a roast dinner. It is called bubble and squeak because of the sounds it makes when being cooked i.e. it bubbles and it squeaks.

The United Kingdom is a Monarchy, which means that a king or queen is head of the state. In the United Kingdom, Queen Elizabeth II is the queen. She is part of the Royal family. She has many homes including Buckingham Palace and Windsor Castle.

The national
anthem of the
United Kingdom
is 'God save
the Queen'

Interesting things

Another popular custom in
the UK is Afternoon Tea. Tea
together with small, neatly
cut sandwiches and scones,
clotted cream and jam are
served. Afternoon tea was
traditionally served to curb
the hunger between lunch
and dinner as dinner was
served late.

Some iconic
sights include
black cabs, big
red busses,
and the red
telephone booths

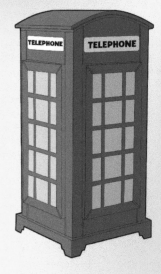

about the United Kingdom

The United Kingdom is an island and has very rainy weather generally, it is not uncommon to see people in their wellies (Wellington boots) and with brollies in hand (shortened word for umbrellas)

London is known for its underground train system called 'The London Underground' and also referred to as the 'Tube'.

UNDERGROUND

My visit to London

Date: _____

_____

_____

_____

_____

_____

_____

_____

_____

FriesenPress

Suite 300 - 990 Fort St
Victoria, BC, V8V 3K2
Canada

www.friesenpress.com

ISBN
978-1-5255-4429-3 (Hardcover)
978-1-5255-4430-9 (Paperback)
978-1-5255-4431-6 (eBook)

1. JUVENILE FICTION, TRAVEL

Distributed to the trade by The Ingram Book Company

CPSIA information can be obtained
at www.ICGtesting.com
Printed in the USA
BVHW020138011119
562622BV00001B/2/P

DATE DUE

PRINTED IN U.S.A.